COOKING THE RICH -
A POST-REVOLUTIONARY
NECESSITY

Cooking the Rich - A post-revolutionary necessity

30 Delicious Recipes

Aaron Aalborg

Penman House
Publishing

Published by Penman House Publishing

ISBN 978-0-9908764-6-5

Typesetting services by BOOKOW.COM

This book is dedicated to 'anthrophagists', cannibals, everywhere. They have realized the true meaning of love for their fellow man.

INTRODUCTION

A rollicking romp through the history of cannibalism

'Nothing more strongly arouses our disgust than cannibalism, yet we make the same impression on Buddhists and vegetarians, for we feed on babies, though not our own.'

- Robert Louis Stevenson

"Oh, I am a cook and a captain bold,
And the mate of the Nancy brig,
And a bo'sun tight, and a midshipmite,
And the crew of the captain's gig"

- W. S. Gilbert - The Yarn of the Nancy Bell

ACKNOWLEDGMENTS

As usual my thanks are due to my wonderful editor, Jenny Kitson, for her excellent work in correcting my atrocios speling, apalling gramor terrible and other torture of the Engwish langwage.

In the case of the recipes, I am in debt to my long-suffering wife and excellent cook Ivy. She is the bravest woman I know, willing to live in close proximity to a homicidal maniac. She it was that supplied most of the recipes, without those essential human ingredients proposed by me.

Those who have read my novels and short stories must be surprised that I decided to write a cookbook. It was the last thing I could have imagined, until I fell under the spell of my gourmet friend, Lenny Karpman.

He has written much of a culinary nature. My favorite is "Foods that confuse and amuse". This book is full of interesting, disgusting and improbable, but real recipes from around the globe. They are accompanied by anecdotes and wit. His works acted as my inspiration and spur, especially as not a single dish he has discovered includes my essential ingredient for a good supper.

His omission is hereby corrected.

"There is nothing more tasty than a human being. The flavor is like that of chicken. The advantage is that there are no tickly feathers."

Sammy, the talking crocodile - personally interviewed by the author, Sydney Zoo 2009.

"Go to the meat market of a Saturday night and see the crowds of live bipeds staring up at the long rows of dead quadrupeds... Cannibals? Who is not a cannibal? I tell you it will be more tolerable for the Fejee that salted down a lean missionary in his cellar against a coming famine; it will be more tolerable for that provident Fejee, I say, in the day of judgement, than for thee, civilized and enlightened gourmand, who nailest geese to the ground and feastest on their bloated livers in thy pate de fois gras."

Herman Melville

Disclaimer

It was a great disappointment to discover from my research that cannibalism is universally illegal among nation states. Self-preservation, motivated lobbying by 19th century colonial missionaries and those who did not value aboriginal cultures, forced their governments to adopt these restrictive rules. This was a travesty of natural justice and showed a lack of respect for others' traditions.

Hopefully at some point in the future, more liberal laws will supersede these archaic constraints. This might require petitions and street demonstrations to encourage the courts to recognize our human right to enjoy tasting other human beings, (other than in the usual way).

One day, we will all be able to delight in eating our enemies, as was perfectly normal in happier and, dare I say it, more civilized times. With your support, 'We shall overcome some day!'

Because of the current law, I have been unable to admit to trying any of the recipes in this book. However, my readings of recorded instances of cannibalism indicate that the dishes herein are viable and likely very tasty. Believe me there is nothing like a succulent, sizzling human rump steak, medium rare, with green pepper sauce. Er, or so I'm told.

Until the law recognizes the right to consume those who deserve it, my legal counsel forces me to advise readers not to actually try these delicious dishes. (She's for the pot one day).

We will see later that after revolutions, law and order break down. Such a happy event might be your only chance to relish these epicurean delights during your lifetime.

A further problem is that parts of this book may be considered treasonous and possibly worse in the UK, Saudi Arabia and Thailand.

Any offensive passages were not written by me, but added by fellow authors. If any murderous hit men, funded by billionaires or other offended parties pay me a visit I will gladly name names for a small honorarium.

Alternatively, my fingers slipped on the keys and as with monkeys randomly banging away at typewriters, the offending pages just happened.

In any event, by the time of publication, I will have moved to live with a cannibal tribe. These warriors live near Mount Hagen in Papua New Guinea. The highland jungles are somewhat impenetrable. These fellows are always ravenous. Do drop in for a visit.

If anyone wants to complain about the efficacy of these recipes before the revolution, please address your complaints directly to the local constabulary, to save me passing the messages on.

Should this book upset anyone, try this recipe. Take one stick of dynamite, sprinkle with sugar and microwave for four minutes. Keep a close watch on the glass door.

CONTENTS

How to use this Book

Some readers may want justification for their next steps towards cannibalism. They can read the introduction in full. Others may wish to dip into various recipes as with any other cookery book.

Anal retentives who delight in reading railway timetables and phone directories are free to digest the whole tome in one go.

Why Cannibalism?

This is not a learned tome on the anthropology and the behavioral psychology of this subject. So, we will just list a series of salient points in logical progression:

1. Evolution has led to pond life, insects, reptiles, birds and animals requiring protein to live.

2. Protein may be consumed from plants or meat.

3. Humans are amongst those beings made of meat.

4. Most of us are omnivorous, preferring to include flesh in our diet, because it contains the highest concentration of protein, essential vitamins and other yummy stuff.

5. Some species happily scoff down humans given the chance. Examples include: bacteria, ants, predatory fish, crocodilians, wolves, bears, lions, tigers, jaguars, crows and vultures.

6. Many species consume their own relatives when need arises or just because they are tasty. The list includes: fungi; many types of fish; insects and worms too numerous to mention; birds such as bitterns and owls; most carnivorous amphibians; reptiles and of course our nearest relatives, chimps. Humans do the same more often than our taboos permit us to believe.

Eating human flesh is forbidden by religion and law in most societies. The same can be said for adultery, murder and theft. However, on occasion these acts are sanctioned by the state, (and can all be tremendous fun in the right circumstances).

We might start to suspect that a good feed on the neighbors could provide as much delight as carnal rumpy-pumpy with attractive members of their households.

Most people are born with an innate fear of being eaten. This derives from a basic survival instinct amongst our early ancestors. Surrounded by wild predators, they had nothing with which to defend themselves except pointy sticks and guile.

Victorian explorers and missionaries, intent on enforcing their beliefs and values across the globe, were shocked to discover rampant cannibalism in many societies. South Sea Islanders, the Dayaks of Borneo, Taiwanese aboriginals and those of New Guinea spring to mind. These estimable warrior peoples felt that by devouring appropriate parts of their bravest enemies, the power of the defeated would transfer to themselves.

Imperialists suppressed such practices, wrote lurid novels about them and fed the prurient interest of the base populace with grisly tales of horror. No self-respecting story of colonial conquest or exploration would sell unless it included a reference to these dark of acts of cuisine or an illustration with a missionary in a cooking pot.

The Victorian and modern obsession with vampires is merely an extension of a related practice. The Kenyan Masai prefer to acquire their protein from fresh blood, drained from their living cattle. Snake's blood, best consumed with vodka or similar spirit to avoid coagulation, is a powerful medicine in Asia. It is the Viagra of the east.

No North Briton can be truly happy without an occasional black pudding, (blood sausage). Any self-respecting Yorkshireman or Lancastrian loves gravy, made from the juices of our own chosen prey. "Why stop there?" asked Idi Amin, Papa Doc Duvalier and other Dracula emulators.

Does all this fascination imply a secret but repressed desire? After all, scrape marks from primitive tools of butchery on human bones dating back thousands of years, are regular finds in European archeological digs.

There are many accounts of those brought up with western taboos who, when hungry, reverted to traditional recipes. Gérichaut's epic painting, 'Le Radeau de la Méduse' (The raft of the Medusa), records one such occasion. The French sailing ship la Méduse went down in a storm. The survivors on the raft did what came naturally. Such tales inspired W.S. Gilbert's 'The Yarn of the Nancy Bell', quoted at the start and end of this volume.

My Irish grandmother assured me that her own grandparents survived the potato famine of 1845 to 1852 by chewing on the dead. Chroniclers attest to these horrors. I am part cannibal, hooray!

Herman Melville, the author of 'Moby Dick', based his novel on verified events. Captain George Pollard Jnr., the captain of the real whaler, returned safely to New England. He apologized to one bereaved mother for eating her son to avoid starvation. She was unforgiving. Some people have no empathy!

In more recent times after an Andean air-crash, starving Argentinean rugby players ate their dead friends. When necessary for survival, the taboos fall away.

In choosing a seat on a plane for flights over empty seas or landscapes, try to sit near someone who looks appetizing. If you want more space, leave a copy of this book on your lap as you snooze. Wait until the plane is airborne. Otherwise the authorities may ground you.

But, why focus on the rich and powerful?

We have proved that eating human flesh is often necessary and sometimes normal in human societies. But why should we select the rich, who rule us, for special treatment?

There is a general consensus that there are too many people on the planet. Seven billion today, with a prospect of ten billion in the near future. This is far too many to be sustainable.

Most scientists concur that global warming, pollution and depletion of vital natural reserves will doom the human race. In

Paris, a weak treaty was recently signed recently for PR purposes. This will not end our merry dance towards self-destruction.

The over-consumption of resources and pollution originated in wealthier countries. It was driven by those striving to be rich. Such wannabes flaunt their possessions, lifestyle and status.

Billionaires and celebrities have become icons to be emulated. Conspicuous and mindless consumption have become their norm. Conned by gossip media, TV soaps and advertising, the masses blindly follow.

Whilst the rich nations literally consume humanity's future, almost a billion men, women and children starve or wake each day with perpetual hunger. 1% of the world's population has accumulated over 90% of the earth's wealth, to be squandered on space tourism, mega yachts, the latest designer labels, luxury cars and other fripperies.

Our solution - By feeding the rich to the deprived, the perpetrators of the problem can be repaid for their profligacy. Simultaneously, the population can be reduced and sustainability restored. Fear of being eaten would be a powerful disincentive against recurrences of greed.

For the hungry, the wealthy are obvious targets. One can safely assume that they live pampered lives. They are therefore more succulent than the skinny and deprived.

During the French Revolution, members of the Paris mob hacked aristocrats and counter-revolutionaries to death. Some of the more excitable sans-culottes ripped out the beating hearts of their victims and scarfed them down raw.

In 1672, Johan de Witt was the Grand Pensionary of Holland, (Equivalent of Prime Minister). He was hacked to death by a mob, dissatisfied with his leadership. Some accounts claim he was eaten in a frenzy of anger.

This book aims to deploy a little more finesse to the removal of the parasites. When should we start? As soon as possible seems to be a good time, revolution first though.

Why are Graces Before Meals Included?

Graces are sprinkled around this culinary masterpiece for three reasons:

1. Though an atheist myself, others may not be. Besides, some of the benedictions might amuse.

2. In most aboriginal societies, the hunters and the shamans gave thanks to the spirit of the animal providing the meat. No thanks are due to the rapacious rich for their carcasses, but hunters, butchers, cooks and vendors deserve our appreciation. Buddhists often meditate on the efforts of the farmers and all those contributing to the provision of a repast.

3. Many graces give thought to those less fortunate, who may not be able to stay their hunger pangs. This empathetic approach is a worthy one.

Choosing your meat

"The Mountain sheep are sweeter
But the valley sheep are fatter;
We therefore deemed it meter
To carry off the latter"

From 'The War-song of Dinas Vawr' by Thomas
Love Peacock

"I have been assured by a very knowing American of
my acquaintance in London, that a young healthy child
well nursed is at a year old a most delicious, nourishing
and wholesome food, whether stewed roasted, baked or
boiled."

Jonathan Swift

Hunting versus the Supermarket

This is not a prescription as to how to overthrow governments
and manage the post-revolutionary process. My novel, *'Rev-*

olution' does that. However, one can take it that the rich will try to hide, especially if they fear being eaten.

It is clearly important to get them all, one way or another. The children of the wealthy and aristocrats seem to have an innate sense of entitlement. Unless every one of them is consumed, they will lead counter-revolutions. We will be back to square one. Besides, ensuring that we get them all will deter others from wishing to be rich, 'pour encourager les autres'.

Many rich people will use their considerable resources to hide and attempt to resist capture. This raises the tricky question of hunting them down.

Throughout the ages, rulers, aristocrats and the affluent have had a penchant for hunting. The British Royal family has hunted and shot its way through thousands of tigers and more recently deer, grouse, pheasants and Afghanis, whilst purporting to support the World Wildlife Fund. (Ha!).

In Africa, the cruel rich mount expensive expeditions to lure endangered animals from game reserves. They massacre them with high-tech weaponry. Their selfies demonstrate a delusion that this is admirable. There seems to be a poetic justice as well as a revolutionary necessity in hunting the well-to-do. But what are the implications of this for choosing your meat?

Hunters for wild food claim that their prey has a gamy flavor. The meat is leaner. It has more muscle. One could expect this to be true for those rich who have been on the run in the wildernesses or who work out a lot.

Bloated capitalists hiding in bunkers may be more marbled. Some cooks may prefer the well-larded who we hope will grace our supermarket shelves. No doubt the label will read 'Free range', 'Fed on caviar and fois gras', or 'Hormone free'.

It would seem more humane to provide these rich people the courtesy of a regular slaughter house. Subjecting them to the terror of the hunt is mean, despite what they did to other beings.

Hunters claim that, as a result of terror, the animals they kill are full of cortisol and other biochemicals. The carcasses need to be hung for a few days. This allows the meat to tenderize and these unwanted flavors to dissipate.

Another issue is that of lead poisoning. If the corpses are riddled with bullets, they may be inedible. One shot to the head with a scoped rifle is the preferred and kindest way to dispatch an oligarch as he crashes through the undergrowth frantic to escape.

Humane verses Halal

The Koran has no apparent prohibition against cannibalism. Perhaps the idea is so outrageous that the Prophet forgot to mention it.

In general, the most painless execution seems best. Whatever fits your religion, so be it.

Can human flesh be kosher?

– Comments from Rabi Streichelngesäß

"God was likely sleeping during past outbreaks of human self-consumption. As a result, little is said about this in the Bible or Talmud.

"My view is that as long as the correct rituals are performed, human flesh is kosher. After all, it isn't pork.

"The Talmud allows cloven-hoofed animals such as goats, sheep and deer. The Scots believe that Satan appears with cloven hooves. We might choose to assume that evil billionaires have such feet. If in doubt, leave their shoes on."

So, which humans should we prefer?

Older people are likely to be tougher, more gristly and difficult to digest. More cooking will be needed. Therefore, the young are better eating than the old.

Sadly, many of the aged rich are hanging on to life, due to superior medical attention. It may be preferable to feast on their trophy wives and offspring whenever possible.

This also avoids ingesting their medications. One cannibal of my acquaintance complained of an erection lasting several days after eating a Viagra-laced oldster. His loved one was delighted though.

CONDITIONING AND BUTCHERY

This section deals with those slaughtered in the same rather unpleasant way we kill cattle, pigs and sheep.

The slaughterhouse process begins with the victims being funneled into the production line. With humans, a mild sedative might help.

They should be 'humanely' stunned, as is meant to be done with animals. The animals are then hauled up by their feet. Their throats are slit by the slaughterer. Some of the throat-slitters get carried away with blood lust. Careful psychiatric screening for this job is advisable.

The meat industry has been described as the car industry in reverse. The carcasses pass down a disassembly line, suspended on a moving chain. Each worker makes one cut, as a carcass passes slowly by. The form of dismemberment depends on the ultimate customer. This varies according to national tradition.

This results in prime steak going to the US for hamburgers. The brains are sent to the Middle East. The lesser cuts, for example tripe and kidneys, are sent to the poorer parts of the world or to the food processing industry. In a more egalitarian world such wasteful transportation could be eliminated and a fair share of the best meat consumed locally.

Curing and Smoking

Humans were known as 'long pig' by South Sea Island cannibals. Our taste is said to be similar to that of pork (contrary to Sammy the croc's opinion). In Islamic and Jewish communities the temptations of bacon can become overwhelming. They therefore use turkey bacon as a substitute. Now there is an alternative. You can eat human turkeys.

As with pork, haunches of human flesh are very suitable for curing or smoking as ham. (You can cure them of their greed if nothing else). This can be done in the same way as for pork. We do not need to cover the process here.

Honey can be smeared over the surface to add sweetness. Studding with cloves gives further flavor. Eating the rich is a sure cure for greed.

Some of the many corpulent rich are a good source of belly bacon. This crisps nicely and is used in one of our dessert recipes.

Special Preparation for Sports Stars

Uber-rich sports stars mock the Olympic ideal, in which the honor of winning and a laurel crown were the only rewards for the victors (probably apart from getting laid a lot). With the exceptions of tiddlywinks champions, sports superstars are clearly within the 1% and firmly on the menu.

Some, like yacht skippers and racing drivers, have normal physiques. They can be prepared in the usual way for the recipes in this book.

It is when we come to the various types of athlete that difficulties arise. As a general rule, they have almost no fat. Obviously this is untrue for Sumo wrestlers.

Some Sumos are rich as Croesus. They marry on retirement. Rumor has it that their diminutive wives are issued with a snorkel for their wedding night. If you are lucky enough to bag one of these mighty Sumo specimens, look on the Internet to see how Africans cook rhinos or hippos as bush meat.

To compensate for the lack of marbling in the meat, other athletes may need basting in butter or soaking in an oily marinade. This will avoid the meat drying out during cooking.

Sports people vary tremendously, Tour De France stars like Bradley Wiggins would make a poor meal, possibly a thin gruel. On the other hand, Junoesque tennis stars like Venus Williams could feed an entire village for a week.

RECIPES FOR EVERY DAY

"When cooking, always use lots of alcohol. Only if absolutely necessary, add it to the food."
Grandma Aalborg

In the following section, we include every-day recipes. We hope you and your family will enjoy them.

Trump a la mode

The Grace: Father Son and Holy Ghost
Who eats the fastest gets the most.

This recipe is especially tricky and strictly for the brave. To really relish this dish invite some of those Mexicans who feel most insulted by Trump's racism.

Preparation

The chef is confronted with a mammoth task. He or she receives a huge, ugly and largely poisonous, wobbling bulk. He has to access any edible parts.

Begin by paring away the 100lbs or so of nauseous fat. This should reveal a nasty little green homunculus. It spits bile as it writhes. 90% of it is venomous ego. The cook may need to break off to be sick when this inner Trump is revealed.

If what remains is considered wholly inedible, it might be best to burn it to avoid poisoning the dogs. Then you can start again, with some of the family.

Footnote -The mass of weird hair can clog the municipal drains. Best to burn it in a furnace at above 1,000 degrees. Bury any ash. To avoid contaminating the water table, ensure that there is a membrane seal under the selected dump.

Ingredients

- 1 Trump head for thickening. No need to remove the brains, there aren't any.
- 3 to 5 pounds of boned Trump short rib
- ½ teaspoon of finely ground nuts. This is fitting as he is completely nuts
- ½ teaspoon of sea salt and another of black pepper
- ¼ pound of cubed Serrano ham
- a medium diced onion
- 2 cups of Barolo. Drink one. Use the other. Hell, just make it three cups and drink two.
- 2 sprigs of fresh thyme, 1 of fresh parsley, 2 bay leaves
- 1 celeriac, chopped coarsely
- 3 carrots, chopped in large pieces
- zest of 1 lemon

Method

Best use long-handled utensils and keep a baseball bat handy. Parts may try to squirm out of the pan.

1. Pat the meat dry with paper towels and rub in the salt, pepper and the nuts.

2. Add the ham to a casserole dish and sauté in a warm oven until the ham is crispy then remove it leaving the rendered fat.

3. Add the meat and brown on both sides till a crust forms.

4. The oven should be preheated to about 180 centigrade. Add the wine. Braise until tender for about 2 hours stirring in the herbs.

5. Add the ham, the carrots, celeriac and stir in with the wine.

6. Remove the meat and ham and simmer the juices.

7. Serve with the juices poured over. Garnish with the lemon zest and some freshly chopped parsley.

Billionaire Bourguignon

The Grace:	Some hae meat and cannae eat,
And some wad eat that want it;
But we hae meat and we can eat,
So let the Lord be thankit.

Attributed to Robert Burns

Some billionaires set up foundations, ostensibly for charitable purposes. Inevitably, these turn out to be scams. They avoid tax. The children of the rapacious rich occupy key positions. They can carry on the family traditions of conspicuous consumption, running for lucrative public office and the like. The Rockefellers and Grosvenors (hereditary Dukes of Westminster), are typical examples. Cooking these dynasties ends the perpetuation of undeserved wealth.

Ingredients

- 2 lbs of billionaire braising steak cut into large chunks. Savor each stroke of the knife remembering the billionaires' former transgressions
- 3 bay leaves
- A small sprig of thyme

- 2 bottles of red wine, unless the billionaire was a heavy drinker. then 1 will do
- 6 medium sized carrots cut into large pieces
- 2 tablespoons of olive oil
- 2 large roughly-chopped onions
- 1 tablespoonful of tomato puree
- ⅓ pound of bacon
- ½ pound of mushrooms
- 6 halved small shallots or onions

To serve - a small knob of butter (Ever wondered whose knob they mean? Just asking.) and chopped parsley.

Method

1. Tip the meat into a large container, with the bay leaves, thyme and wine. Add ground pepper, cover and leave in the fridge overnight.

2. Pre heat the oven to 200C.

3. Strain the meat through a large colander retaining the wine.

4. Heat half the oil in a big frying pan and brown the meat in batches and keep to one side. When this is done pour the wine into the frying and warm till it bubbles.

5. Using a large casserole dish, fry the carrots and onion till they begin to color in the rest of the oil. Stir in the tomato puree. Add the meat, wine, herbs and seasoning. Bake for two hours in the oven until the meat is very tender.

6. To serve, warm the butter in a frying pan, add the bacon and shallots and fry for about 10 minutes. Stir in the mushrooms and fry for about five minutes. Stir everything into the stew and add chopped parsley.

Bankers' Hearts

They had no grace and deserve none.

The Romans considered both larks' tongues and dormice to be haute cuisine. Presumably, the small size of each morsel added to its perceived value.

When dining with Chinese, the whole fish is served with the head facing the guest of honor. The one so favored is expected to relish the cheeks and lips. Sorry to say that fish are mostly deficient in these tasty areas. Extracting what little there is with chopsticks is a tricky and unrewarding process. Perhaps it is intended to reveal the ineptitude of the Guilo guests (White Devils).

With these delicacies in mind, a meal of bankers' hearts seemed a good addition to our recipes. At least three will be needed for each serving, as they are so small. They are also very hard. In many cases veritably stony. If necessary, treble the cooking time. Or give them a good thrashing with a mallet. With each blow, think of the time you were turned down for a loan.

Ingredients

- At least 3 hearts per person. Serve with mashed potatoes, a vegetable and horseradish sauce.

Method

1. Slice the hearts in two. Further division will make the pieces too small to see.

2. Grill, barbeque or fry over a high heat for 4 minutes.

Murdoch stew

The Grace: Crunch, crunch! Gulp!

Sammy, the talking crocodile

This is a difficult dish, not to be attempted by beginners. Apart from being skinny, gristly and old, there are huge quantities of nasty toxins throughout the meat. The spleen comprises half the body weight.

Careful preparation is needed initially to remove the head from up the anus. Next, one needs to ensure all the poison is removed. This is best attempted by a licensed blowfish chef from Japan. These chefs are used to dealing with such potentially deadly items.

On balance, it might be best to toss the patriarchal Murdoch aside and feast on the extended family or mistresses. Given the provenance of this dynasty, we have adapted a kangaroo recipe.

Ingredients

- 1 tablespoon olive oil
- ¾ pound of Murdoch fillet
- ¼ cup salt and ground black pepper

- ¾ pound of pumpkin, skinned and diced into ¼ inch cubes
- 2 medium diced zucchini
- 1 peeled and diced red onion
- 6 cloves of garlic with the skin intact
- ⅓ cup extra virgin olive oil
- ¼ cup of balsamic vinegar
- 2 tablespoons of chopped mint
- 1 cup of couscous
- 2 cups of hot vegetable stock
- ¼ cup of chopped coriander
- Juice of 1 lemon
- 1 cup of crumbled feta
- ¼ cup of chopped almonds

Method

1. Preheat the oven to 300F.

2. Place the pumpkin, zucchini, garlic, two tablespoons of olive oil, onion, and vinegar in a large roasting pan. Season with salt and pepper and place in the oven for 30 minutes, turning at least once.

3. For the couscous heat 1 tablespoon of olive oil and vinegar in a large saucepan over medium heat. Add the couscous

and cook for 3 to 4 minutes or until lightly browned. Pour in the vegetable stock, reduce the heat and cook for 15 minutes or until the stock is soaked up. Stir occasionally.

4. For the Murdoch meat, heat the remaining oil in a frying pan. Rub the meat with the salt. Brown the meat on all sides in the pan. Take the meat and place it on the baking tray. Cook in the oven for 10 minutes and then cut into thin slices.

5. Toss the meat in a large mixing bowl with the couscous, mint, coriander and lemon juice. Top off with the feta and almonds.

Hearty Gold Bug Hot Pot

The Grace: Good food, good meat,
                    Good Lord, let's eat.

You have likely met gold bugs at parties. They usually rant on about the imminent collapse of paper currency, how gold always gains in value and how they were clever enough to buy when it was only a dollar a ton. Most of these people are full of BS. Successful investors do not attend parties with the likes of us. They hold their parties on their mega yachts in Monaco.

Still, if you really want to eat gold bugs, the BS types you meet will do at a pinch. The others will be tracked down and slaughtered in their luxury surroundings.

Ingredients

- 1½ pounds of boneless gold bug loin cut into 1 inch cubes
- 3 medium carrots cut into large slices
- ½ cup chopped onion
- ½ cup of diced butternut squash
- 4 cups chicken or vegetable stock
- ½ cup diced parsnips of squash
- 1 teaspoon of mixed salt and pepper
- 3 tablespoons of flour

- 3 tablespoons of softened butter
- A pinch of gold dust for irony. Gold leaf is used in exotic foods and drinks. The vodka based Goldwasser from Gdansk is a classic example, with floating gold leaf. It would be a fitting accompaniment to this dish.

Method

1. Put all ingredients except the flour and butter into a slow cooker.

2. Cover and cook on low heat for 7 hours.

3. Mix the flour and butter into small balls and add them to the stew. Stir well.

4. Cook on high heat for 35 minutes, stirring when needed.

5. Sprinkle the gold dust on top for a rich meal.

Fat Cat Fricassee

The Grace: A rich man is one who has his next meal
before him.

The Buddha

The greedy chief executives and chairpersons of major cor-
porations sit on one another's boards. They determine each
other's pay and perks. Their hidden benefits, such as private
boxes at sports and cultural events; use of executive jets; corporate apartments in holiday locations and massive severance
bonuses, rarely appear in published accounts.

For some reason these fat cats feel entitled to the bulk of the rewards for an enterprise's success. They forget that many people
are essential to success; from the cleaner to the designer; from
the manufacturer to the packer; from the shipper to the sales
rep.

CEOs and Chairpersons should appear on any respectable so-
cialist menu. They are brave when firing others, but cowardly
otherwise. We have therefore substituted them for chicken in
this recipe.

Ingredients

- ¾ pound of prime fat cat rump sliced into 1inch thick
  slices.

- A medium sliced onion
- ½ cup of mushrooms
- ¼ cup of flour
- 1 glass of dry white wine, 2 or more if you intend to drink some
- ½ cup of chicken stock
- 2 tablespoons of butter
- 1/cup of double cream. As always, Fat Cats get the cream!
- 1 teaspoon of cumin and Salt and pepper

Method

1. Coat the sliced meat in flour.

2. Dice the mushrooms and onion.

3. Warm butter in a frying pan and gently cook the onions until soft.

4. Add the mushrooms and cook for 3 minutes.

5. Add the meat and cook till brown all over.

6. Add the white wine, the cumin and salt and pepper.

7. Add the chicken stock, bring to the boil and simmer for 20 minutes.

8. Serve on a bed of rice, pouring the double cream over the meal

Koch au Vin

The Grace: We are needy. They were greedy.
Make them into a jolly feedy.

The Koch brothers are among the richest of all billionaires. Their attempts to buy electoral and legislative influence with hundreds of millions of dollars are widely reported. They support extreme right wing policies.

Beat them with a tenderizing mallet, as they are old and gristly. (When they are dead of course. Mustn't be cruel, unless you feel they deserve it).

Ingredients

1. pieces of Koch,

2. Half a liter of white plonk. They do not deserve the best.

3. Slices of aubergine and other suitable veggies.

4. Herbs, salt and pepper.

Method

Cook over a slow heat in a covered casserole dish for 3 hours.

Serve with mashed potatoes.

Kardashian Sausage Cassoulet

The Grace: A hundred hairy savages
sitting down to lunch.
Gobble gobble glup glup,
Munch munch munch

Some male readers must have looked upon a callipygous woman and been tempted to take a bite. Empathy prevails and most of us do not indulge. If anyone bit a Kardashian, it might be like chewing on an inflatable floatation device.

If you cannot get a genuine Kardashian, there are lots of other pointless and vacuous celebs to choose from. Just pick one from the tabloids or talk shows.

Care is needed to remove the various large implants from the buttocks, breasts and lips. This reduces the volume by about 50% and results in a rather floppy carcass.

The resulting real Kardashian that this reveals will not be a pretty sight. Do not worry, cooking will soon remove this unpleasant spectacle.

It is important to remove the skin. It will be seeped in unpleasant oils and chemicals from trowelling on makeup.

The resulting meat is nearly as tasteless as the Kardashians themselves. It is best to have it made into Toulouse-style sausages. This will spice them up. They will be far more interesting than they ever were in life.

Ingredients

- 8 Kardashian Toulouse sausages
- 1 ½ cups of green lentils
- 2 tablespoons each of olive oil, sherry vinegar and freshly chopped parsley
- a knob of butter
- 1 finely chopped onion
- 2 diced garlic cloves
- 1 medium finely chopped carrot
- 1 bay leaf
- 1 stick of finely chopped celery
- 4 rashers of diced smoked bacon
- ½ a chopped leek
- 3 cups of beef stock
- 2 cups of red wine
- 2 shredded ducks legs

Method

1. Brown the sausages in butter and oil.

2. Heat a sauté pan adding the knob of butter and two table-spoons of olive oil. Once hot add the onion and cook for 2 minutes. Then add the garlic and diced bacon, carrot, leek, bay leaf and cook for 2 more minutes.

3. Add the lentils and wine, cook until the wine is reduced by ½ and add the stock. Mix in the vinegar and parsley.

4. Mix in the duck and sausages and cook for 28 minutes.

5. Serve with pureed potatoes and double cream.

Sammy the Dayak's Planter Curry

The Grace: Plant a planter in the pot.
Cook him well and serve him hot.

After a long and steamy trek through the Borneo rainforest, I shared a delicious spicy meal with Sammy, our Dayak guide, in his longhouse. In retrospect, I wonder what the meat was.

He told me that in the colonial era, the British exploited the indigenous peoples from the Indian subcontinent and Borneo. The tea and palm oil planters ruled their petty kingdoms as though they were gods. They made free with the local girls, whipped men and women into submission and lived the life of kings. The headhunting Dayaks developed this recipe for those that strayed too far into the jungle. Any member of the 1% will do for this recipe.

Ingredients

- 5 peeled and chopped shallots
- 2 tablespoons of ground nut oil
- 2 peeled and crushed cloves of garlic
- 2 inches of freshly ground ginger root
- 1 tablespoon each of curry powder, ground coriander, chili powder, ground cinnamon

- 1 star anise
- 5 cloves
- 2 lbs of rich person loin steak cut into 1-inch cubes
- 2 large red chilies with the seeds removed.
- 1lb of potatoes
- ½ teaspoon of sea salt
- ⅓ cup of coconut milk
- 1 teaspoon of soft brown sugar
- 2 red chilies diced to garnish
- 2 tablespoons of fresh lime juice

Method

1. Heat the nut oil in a large pan and gently fry the garlic, ginger and shallots for 4 minutes.

2. Add the curry powder, chili powder, cinnamon, coriander, star anise and cloves. Fry for a further minute.

3. Add the meat and stir to coat in the spice mixture. Add the potatoes, chopped chilies, salt and coconut milk and bring to the boil. Cover the pan and simmer for 45 minutes, stirring until the meat is tender. Prior to serving add the lime juice and sugar and stir. Cook without the lid for 3 minutes.

4. Serve with basmati rice and mango chutney

Senator Hamburgers

The Grace: He graced the senate seat
Long after he was able.
Now he provides our meat and
graces our modest table.

Senators are usually fatty enough to require grilling as hamburger. Those of a cruel disposition might want to keep them alive as they are fed through the mincer to atone for their past, self-serving deeds.

It is important that the butcher gives you meat from the right end. Senators usually talk through their butts, which can cause confusion.

You may need to add spices to take away the residual taste of corruption. Then, they will be finger-licking good.

Ingredients

- 3lbs of lean minced senator will make 12 4oz burgers
- 2 whisked eggs for binding
- 3 cloves of chopped garlic
- ½ teaspoonful each of sea salt and ground black pepper
- Chili sauce to taste

Method

1. Mix the ingredients and form into burgers of the size and thickness you prefer. Senators all got their hands dirty, but you may not wish to taint yours, so use disposable food gloves.

2. Cook on the barbeque.

3. Serve with hamburger buns and add whatever relishes you prefer.

Plutocrat meatballs, with real balls – a dish from Taiwan

The Grace: Cantonese, Fukianese, Hainanese.
Good grief, what are these?
I refuse to eat that.

The remaining 500,000 aborigines from Taiwan, formerly Formosa, have done well to survive. In the past, many were headhunters. Maybe some still are. This recipe was gifted to me by a like-minded friend from the Atayal ethnic group during a visit.

Formosa was invaded by the Chinese various times, then by the Japanese and finally (so far) by Chiang Kai-shek's Kuomintang forces fleeing from the victorious communists on mainland China. Each invasion led to ill-treatment of the locals.

The Chinese are not known for wasting any animal protein. Ducks' feet, scorpions and dogs are all on the menu in China. During my research I came across accounts of the Chinese invaders eating the Formosan aboriginals and even exporting some of their parts as delicacies to the mainland. Apparently, the soles of the feet, kidneys and heart were especially prized.

There are lots of Chinese billionaires, especially in Hong Kong, Taipei, Shanghai and Beijing. It seems only fair that they should have their very own recipe. (If anyone wants to try this, please do not invite me.)

Ingredients

- 1 pair of testicles per serving

- lemon juice

- 2 teaspoonfuls each of soy sauce and palm oil

- Half a cup of rice wine. (Best drink a whole bottle first, if you are going to eat this stuff.)

- 1 teaspoonful of sesame oil

- salt and black pepper

Method

1. Rub the balls with sesame oil and salt and pepper. (The billionaire should be dead first. Why should he get to enjoy this?)

2. Heat the palm oil in a wok till it is really hot and add the soy sauce. Stir the testicles till they are brown all over with a crust. Apparently they may burst during this process. (Yuk!)

3. Reduce the temperature and pour in the wine. Simmer for 5 minutes.

4. Add the lemon juice and serve with boiled rice and baby bok choy or other green vegetable (you will go green too.)

Johnnie from Irian Jaya's Oligarch Rendang

The Grace: Hunting in the dark,
caught an oligarch.
Thank you god of thunder.
Don't let him make me chunder.

I have such happy memories of life in what used to be known as New Guinea. This is probably because I have never been there. Johnnie the Mudman, from Irian Jaya, is my latest invisible friend. We often share a wee dram with my other friends, Johnny Walker, Glen Morangie and Jack Daniels. The Mudmen fashion masks from river ooze, in memory of ancestors who evaded enemies and consequent ingestion by hiding in the mud of a sacred river.

At the end of World War Two, the colonialist Americans decided to abolish the Dutch colonies and implant regimes more to their own liking. With their typical ineptitude, they created the 3,000 mile-long archipelago of Indonesia. This mashed together Christians, Hindus, Muslims and pagans into a combustible mix.

None of these groups had any cultural relationship to each other. As a result, the pro-communist Sukarno seized power, the opposite of what the geniuses in the State Department had envisaged. The other cultures were invaded and subsumed by corrupt Javanese under the subsequent, US supported, fascist Suharto regime.

When Indonesia was created, what was formerly known as 'New Guinea' was divided between Indonesia, as 'Irian Jaya' and the independent state of Papua New Guinea. The terrain and topography is such that the headhunting tribes still survive in their deep jungle retreats.

Rendang is a typical South East Asian dish.

Ingredients

- 1 finely chopped onion
- 1 table spoon each of: galangal, fresh ginger, chopped garlic, tamarind paste and turmeric
- 2 tablespoons of sunflower oil
- 1 cinnamon stick
- ! lemon grass stalk tough part removed and finely chopped
- 6 long dried chilies
- 6 cardamom pods
- kafirr lime- 4 leaves and zest of one fruit
- 1 and a half pound of Oligarch steak cut into 2 inch cubes
- 15 fluid ounces of coconut milk
- coriander sprigs to garnish

Method

1. Blend the onion, ginger, galangal, garlic, lemongrass, turmeric and chilies in a food processor to a smooth

puree.

2. Heat the wok and add the oil. Fry the paste over high heat until it turns darker and aromatic.

3. Crush the cardamom pods and add them. Break the cinnamon stick in two, add and cook for 1 minute.

4. Add the meat stirring all the time, until it is well browned.

5. Pour over the coconut milk and tamarind puree, bring to a simmer, add the kaffir lime zest and leaves. Season with salt and stir. Cook for 1½ hours.

6. Serve with boiled rice.

Oil Baron, Guinness and Oyster pie

The Grace: Please bless this food.
It needs all the help it can get.

This pie should become another favorite, especially for pub food served with fries. As an alternative, serve a roast, Baron of Oil Baron.

When you surgically remove the Stetson, you may find that there is not much left, except a pile of pistols and hollow point ammunition. If this is not the case, you can proceed as below.

If no oil barons are available, you can use members of the Guinness dynasty to complement the nutty, stout flavoring.

Ingredients

- 3 tablespoons of olive oil
- 1 tablespoon of butter
- ½ pound of oil baron steak cut into bite sized chunks
- 5 whole shallots
- ¼ pound of lardons of smoked bacon
- 2 finely chopped onions
- 2 finely chopped garlic cloves
- 1½ pints of Guinness or other stout.

- A glass of red wine
- A glass of Madeira
- 8 oysters
- ⅓ pound of ready-to-roll puff pastry
- 1 egg lightly beaten
- Thyme

Method

1. Heat the oil in a large casserole dish and fry the steak until browned all over. Remove the steak.

2. Add the butter to the pan and fry the shallots for 4 minutes.

3. Add bacon, thyme and onions and cook for 3 minutes. Add the Guinness and the meat.

4. Stir in the garlic, red wine and Madeira and cook slowly for 1 hour 30 minutes.

5. Stir in the oysters.

6. Set the oven at 200C. Roll the pastry and cover the top of the casserole. Paint with the egg and bake for 30 minutes, until the pasty rises and is golden brown.

Special Delights for Holy Days and Feast Days

"Religion is excellent stuff for keeping common people quiet. Religion is what keeps the poor from murdering the rich"

Napoleon Bonaparte

Celebration of Religious Holidays

Marx labeled religion as *'The opiate of the masses'*. In reality it is much worse. Wars of religion have divided humanity since before written history.

In order to give some meaning to the life of drudgery of the peasantry, the great lie of eternal life was spawned. It was an easy confidence trick. Lack of scientific explanation of everyday phenomena such as eclipses, the seasons and the rising of the sun and moon, made the lower orders easy marks, ripe for exploitation.

Brutal rulers were able to legitimize their oppression by appealing to mankind's spiritual nature. In all cases, the authority of the said rulers was boosted by a priestly and educated class. The high priests were often related to the rulers. It was a simple matter to equate rule with divine appointment.

These loathsome clergy wormed their way into positions of power. They were thus able to enrich and give status to themselves as well as support to their ruling relatives.

Think of Archbishop Odo, half-brother of William the Conqueror. He is depicted in the Bayeux Tapestry in full armor at the Battle of Hastings. He wields a huge knobby club, intended to batter his victims to the ground. Not carrying a sword preserved the fiction of his care for his fellow man. After the conquest, large swathes of England were ceded to him including the manor of Gayhurst. This featured in my book *Revolution*.

There are other examples from every society and from every era, from Ancient Egypt to Benin, from the Aztecs and Incas to the Borgias. The clergy's influence was bloody, licentious and evil.

Today, we have religious massacres and strife on a continuing basis in the Middle East, Africa, the Americas and parts of Europe. Priests well deserve their inclusion in the volume.

Still, people like celebrating so it is fitting and proper to continue doing so with the deceitful priesthoods still playing a key role.

Fajitos De Cardinale

The Grace: You wore a red hat.
You were a fat cat.
Now we going to eat you.
How about that?

My novel, *They deserved it*, included several nasty, greedy and randy princes of the Roman Church.

This recipe is highly recommended. Catholics can hardly complain. The central rite of their mass is an act of cannibalism.

As a side benefit of this recipe, you might come by a nice red outfit with a broad brimmed scarlet hat too.

Italians must already be thinking along these lines, as the long twisted pasta, strozzapreti, translates as priest strangler.

Ingredients

Marinade

- 1/ cup of olive oil
- ½ teaspoon of each: fresh lime juice, coarsely ground black pepper, dried oregano, salt
- 2 crushed garlic cloves
- 2 cups of beef broth
- 2 tablespoons of Worcester sauce

Fajitas

- 1 pound of cardinal flank steak
- 1 boned skinned chicken breast
- 2 red bell peppers cut into 12 wedges
- 2 green bell peppers cut into larger wedges
- 1 chopped sweet onion
- 16 6-inch tortillas
- 1 cup salsa
- ¼ cup of sour cream
- ½ cup chopped cilantro
- Fresh cilantro sprigs

Method

1. For the marinade, combine the first ten ingredients in a bowl and set aside.

2. For the fajitas, score the steak in a diamond pattern on both sides and combine this and the chicken with ½ the marinade, seal in a zip lock back and store in the fridge for 4 hours.

3. Combine the remaining marinade with the vegetables and keep refrigerated for 4 hours.

4. Remove the steak and peppers from the marinade. Reduce the marinade in a small saucepan.

5. Grill the meat and peppers on each side for 8 minutes.

6. Wrap the tortillas tightly in foil and add to the grill for the last 2 minutes.

7. Cut the meat diagonally into strips across the grain. Lay the meat and peppers on the tortillas and wrap with cream, salsa and cilantro at the top end. Garnish with cilantro sprigs.

8. Chant "Do this in memory of me."

Ayatollah Pepperoni and Couscous

The Grace: Oh Allah bless the food you have
provided us and save us from the
punishment of hell fire in the
name of Allah.

Misogynous hate-preachers in Iran deserve to be eliminated. This Middle Eastern dish is an appropriate and delightful way to do this.

Ingredients

- 1 large red onion cut into wedges
- ¼ pound of cherry tomatoes
- 1 large aubergine cut into pieces
- 8 chopped ayatollah and herb pepperoni sausages
- 3 tablespoons of olive oil
- 1 cup of couscous
- 2 cups of heated chicken stock
- I juiced lemon
- ¼ pound of green beans

Method

1. Preheat the oven to 180 F. Place the aubergine, onion, tomatoes and sausages in a large roasting tin. Drizzle with 2/3 of the olive oil, season and roast for 25 minutes, turning twice.

2. Meantime, put the couscous in a bowl and stir in the rest of the olive oil. Pour over the chicken stock and cover to stand for 10 minutes. Fluff up the grains with a fork, stirring in the lemon.

3. Blanch the green beans in boiling water for 2 minutes, then cool with cold water.

4. Take the roasting pan from the oven, mix the contents with the green beans and serve.

Megachurch Leader Chili

The Grace: We used snakes for faith healing.
Now we're steaks and more appealing.

You have all seen their saccharine appeals for donations on TV in the name of 'The Lord'. That is how they fund their tax-free private planes, strings of mistresses and expensive lifestyles.

From time to time, they are caught out in their hypocrisy. Then they tearfully confess to their sins and are duly forgiven to carry on as before. They deserve to be cooked for their exploitation of simple folks' need to believe in a higher power.

Ingredients

- 3 pounds of cubed megachurch leader chuck steak
- 4 ounces of chopped bacon
- 1 diced onion
- 4 cloves of sliced garlic
- ¼ cup of minced jalapenos
- 1 bottle of beer
- 2 tablespoons each of: brewed Costa Rican coffee, cornmeal
- ¼ cup of unsweetened cocoa

- One can of plum tomatoes
- 1 cup beef broth
- ½ cup of molasses
- 1 tablespoon each of: oregano, black pepper, chili powder, cumin and salt

Method

1. Preheat the oven to 380 degrees. Meanwhile render the bacon in a dutch oven and set it aside.

2. Brown the meat all over in the bacon grease and set aside.

3. Add the garlic, jalapenos and onion and lightly brown. Add all the other ingredients together and stir.

4. Place the dutch oven in the oven and cook stirring 4 times for 3 to 4 hours until the meat is tender.

5. Serve in a large bowl with cornbread.

In unison shout "Alleluia, Praise be".

Recipes for Special Occasions

The Aristocratic Collection and Appropriate Toasts
"Men will never be free until the last king is strangled with the entrails of the last priest"
Denis Diderot

Why Eat Monarchs?

The royal PR machines persuade the sheeple that unelected monarchs and their extended families are benign, hardworking, and loving of the poor and needy. Their life styles belie this.

Nothing can hide the ridiculous anachronism of an unelected elite playing even a symbolic role in modern governments.

The British Royals have spawned innumerable offspring to help them milk their enraptured British, Dominion and Commonwealth dupes. There still may not be enough of them to feed the millions of starving. In this case, other strutting and undeserving petty German, Spanish, Thai, Dutch, Bruneian or Scandinavian aristocrats may be substituted. One suspects that they all taste the same.

Real Windsor Soup

The Grace: Windsor soup was her favorite dish.
We'd rather eat her than dine on fish.

Windsor soup was a favorite of Queen Victoria. Some say that the British Empire was built on this soup. It must have been named after the Castle rather than her German family name.

The British Royals are always ready to do anything to keep their unjustified position. In World War One, King George V changed the family name from Saxe-Coburg and Gotha to Windsor. This was just as well as Gotha bombers were terrifying Londoners around that time.

In atonement for those of many races slaughtered, enslaved and subjected by the soldiers of the Queen, past and present, it only seems fair that the Windsors should provide the essential ingredient for our soup.

Ingredients

- Two tablespoons of butter (English of course)
- ¼ pound of stewing steak from a royal scrounger
- ¼ pound of mutton
- 4 cups of beef stock
- 1 sliced onion

- 1 sliced carrot
- 1 sliced parsnip
- 2 tablespoons of flour
- 1 bouquet garni
- ¼ teaspoon of chili powder
- ½ cup of cooked rice
- ¼ cup of Madeira wine

Method

1. Cube the lamb and Windsor meat.

2. Brown the butter in a saucepan and fry the meat for 3 minutes and stir in the flour and fry until it is golden brown. Add the chili powder.

3. Add the vegetables and stir in the stock. Drop in the bouquet garni. Partially cover and simmer for 2 hours stirring occasionally.

4. Puree the soup before adding the rice.

5. Serve piping hot and stir in the Madeira at the table. (This was formerly done by a flunky, but if you have one you might end up in the next batch of soup, so best to do it yourself.)

Roast Royal buttock

The Grace: For good Friends, good Fun, good Food and all the other good Fs in life.

Attributed to King Charles II

Most aristocrats sit on their butts while others work. These much kissed and pampered body parts should make a great roast.

Ingredients

- 3 pounds of royal butt steak
- 4 tablespoons of olive oil
- ½ pound of mushrooms
- 2 quartered small onions
- 1 cup of red wine
- 1 cup of beef stock
- 2 spoonfuls of cornflour
- salt and pepper

Method

1. Preheat the oven to 375F, season the meat with salt and pepper to taste.

2. Heat 2 tablespoons of oil in a large iron skillet over medium heat till hot but not smoking. Add the meat and sear on all sides.

3. Season and add the mushrooms and onions to a bowl and stir in the rest of the oil. Add to the skillet around the roast.

4. In the oven, roast until the meat thermometer reads 130F, about 40 minutes. Remove and put the meat on a cutting board.

5. Whilst the meat is resting, prepare the gravy by putting the skillet on a low heat. Add the wine and the stock, scraping the browned bits from the bottom. Whisk in the flour until it is thickened and smooth.

6. Serve with potatoes and vegetables of your choice.

Duke of Wellington Wellington

The Grace: Wellington boots are chewy and tough.
Let our meat be tender enough.

Beef Wellington is one of my favorite dishes. There are many landed aristocrats in the UK and elsewhere that inherited their titles and wealth from long-dead ancestors. Here is a mouth-watering way to end this entirely stupid tradition.

The current Wellesleys are far removed from the Iron Duke. He became a monster, unleashing his troops to sabre down the poor peaceful protesters and their families at St. Peter's fields in Manchester in 1819, 'Peterloo'. I hope that my ancestors were there, agitating and that I or my descendants will exact retribution by eating this dish.

Ingredients

- Fillet(s) from the current Wellingtons, about 2¼ pounds
- 3 tablespoons of olive oil
- 8 ounces of wild mushrooms
- 3 ounces of butter
- 2 sprigs of thyme
- 14 slices of Parma ham
- 1 ¼ pounds of puff pastry

- Salt and ground black pepper
- 2 egg yolks beaten with a teaspoonful of milk
- ½ cup of Cabernet Sauvignon

Method

1. Heat the oven to 175F. Season the meat with salt and pepper, place it on a roasting tray and lightly coat with olive oil. Roast for 20 minutes. Remove and allow to cool before chilling in the fridge for 30 minutes.

2. Chop the mushrooms and add the thyme. Fry them with the butter and rest of the olive oil, till they are slightly soft.

3. Add the wine and cook till it is absorbed.

4. Remove the thyme and set the mushroom aside to cool.

5. Place the ham so it covers the middle of a piece of waxed paper, cover with the mushrooms. Place the fillet on top and wrap it with the ham and mushroom, making a sausage shape.

6. Roll out the pastry and place the meat in the middle, wrapping it in the pastry. Glaze it with the egg yolk.

7. Cook in the oven till it is a golden colour and allow to cool before slicing to serve.

Carpaccio Faisal

The Grace: We pray that what is in this tea pot
is not tea but rather G&T
like you used to drink.

The Saudi Royals number thousands. Their patronymics tend to sound like this, Abu bin Faisal, bin the trash, where's you bin, al Saud.

Forget Lawrence of Arabia's romanticism. The Saudis rule ruthlessly as feudal kings over an unequal, female-suppressing and fanatical society. Their prisoners are tortured and public beheadings are common.

The large supply of royal carcasses, due to multiple wives and hordes of little princes and princesses should make this a popular dish. Inshallah.

Ingredients

- 10 ounces of tenderloin from the royal family
- 4 handfuls of mixed green vegetables
- Vinaigrette
- Sea salt and black pepper
- Parmesan cheese

Method

1. Cook the meat wrapped loosely in foil in an oven at 175F for two hours.

2. Slice into pieces and lay out on plastic wrap.

3. Beat each slice with a mallet till wafer thin. Place on chilled serving plates.

4. Toss the greens with the vinaigrette.

5. Add salt and pepper and dust with the cheese.

Duchess with Duchesse potatoes

The Grace: Her grace the Duchess of York
looks like a carcass of pork.
Let us pray that she tastes the same.

If real duchesses are scarce, feel free to use a countess, baroness or some other titled lay-about. If you are lucky enough to find that they swallowed their jewels to hide them from the vengeful mob, keep quiet about it. You may become food yourself. Besides, carrots are so much more digestible than carats.

Ingredients

- 3 pounds of peeled and cubed large potatoes
- 2 knobs of butter
- ½ teaspoon each of ground nutmeg, salt and black pepper
- 3 egg yolks
- Spraying oil
- 1 pound of your favorite cut of Duchess steak, cooked as you like it

Method

1. Boil the potatoes until tender.

2. Drain and heat gently until the steam stops.

3. Heat the oven to 450F. Cover a baking tray with baking paper. Add a knob of butter, nutmeg salt and pepper and mash the potatoes until smooth in the pan. Stir in the eggs and make small separate piles on the tray. Twirl the tops with a spoon.

4. Spray with oil and bake for 18 minutes.

5. Serve with the meat and your choice of salad or green vegetables.

Real Cock o'Leekie soup

The Toast: Incoming food! Grace! Grace!

From a submarine's mess

We included this heart-warming winter dish in recognition of what the Scottish land-owning aristocracy gave to their fellow countrymen. To this day they own vast estates, initially given for service to foreign conquerors.

Some betrayed their own clansmen by fighting on the English side in various wars. If it were not for them, Scotland would already be independent of the farcical rule from remote Westminster.

Others cleared their poor tenants from their lands, burning the roofs of their crofts, even selling their laborers into colonial indentured servitude. Sheep replaced their hungry and abused families.

The best thing about this recipe is that it will stop these braying aristocrats with their English accents from breeding. Into the pot with them!

Ingredients

- The boned forearm or calf of a lairdie

- Pepper and salt
- 2 peeled and diced carrots
- A large stick of chopped celery
- 2 large chopped onions
- 2 chopped leeks
- 1 minced clove of garlic
- 1 bouquet garni
- 15 pitted dates
- 3 egg whites

Method

1. Heat the oven to 400F. Place the meat in a rack over a roasting dish and roast for 25 minutes until golden brown.

2. Put the meat in a large pan and cover with water, add the garlic and bouquet garni and boil for 1 hour or until tender.

3. Cut the meat into small pieces. Add back the stock from the roasting dish.

4. Blanch the leeks and drain in chilled water.

5. Clarify the stock and coat the meat with the egg.

6. Add all the ingredients and simmer for 10 minutes.

TOASTS

The cellars of aristocratic households include many prized vintages. These make a fitting accompaniment to that special meal.

Here are some appropriate toasts for these feasts.

"You lorded over us, starred in the royal soaps paid for with our money and now you are soup."

"You were arbiters of taste and now we taste you."

"So end all undeserving bloodsuckers."

When eating Scottish lairds,

"Here's ti us and to hell with the English."

For Middle Eastern and Brunei potentates,

"For all the women you have subjugated and all those you have murdered and tortured. Revenge!"

Let Nothing Go to Waste

'Waste not, want not.'

An old proverb

"1 in 7 people go to sleep hungry"

Oxfam

Tripe and onion stew

In western society we throw away far too much food.

When I was small, no part of an animal ever went to waste. The intestines were used for sausage skins. Hooves, bones and the like went to the glue factory. Hides and skins went to make leather. We should do the same with the rich.

Mother used to buy tripe, cow heals and pigs trotters at the long gone UCP (United Cattle Products) shop. You can make tripe from the rich. Many of them talk tripe, so they deserve to be so used. Besides, their stomachs will be especially succulent, distended and pampered by the very best cuisine and fine wines.

Ingredients

- 3 pounds of dressed tripe
- 2 pounds of onions
- 1 pint of milk
- Pepper and salt
- A knob of butter
- 2 ounces of cornflour

Method

1. Cut the tripe in to 3 inch pieces. Boil in water and simmer for 20 minutes.

2. Pour away the water and add the milk, and chopped onions.

3. Melt the butter and mix in the cornflour. Add the milk from the tripe to make the sauce. Season and pour over the tripe. Reheat.

Jellied Oligarch's Head

Some headhunters removed the bones and shrunk the heads.
This recipe was inspired by my mother's recipe for dealing with
a sheep's head.

Ingredients

- 1 skinned oligarch's head
- Salt, pepper, rosemary and thyme
- Gelatin

Method

1. Put the entire head in a very large pan, cover with water,
   add salt and pepper and boil for 7 hours on a medium
   heat.

2. Allow to cool. Skim off the fat from the top. Then remove all flesh and brains discarding the skull and the eyes
   if they bother you.

3. Add the meat back into a fresh pan and again cover with
   water, season with the herbs and add a little pepper.

4. Add sufficient gelatin to solidify the water and put the lot
   into a large mould. Allow to cool and put in the fridge.

5. Tip out and serve cold in slices, with a salad and bread.

Rather disgusting, but nourishing.

Uses for Bones

Educational uses for bones

Every classroom in every school should have a human skeleton. This can do double duty.

It can help to teach anatomy. It can also serve well in cookery classes to illustrate where the various joints of meat come from.

In teaching social and political history, nothing is as memorable as a dismembered skeleton of a former ruler.

Agricultural Use

In former times of plenty, Massachusetts farmers spread lobsters on their fields as fertilizer. In some parts of the world fishmeal and krill still serve the same purpose.

The ground bones of the rich could add calcium to enrich the soil.

Drinking Vessels

A somewhat eccentric friend of mine, (what other sort would you expect me to have?), quaffs his wine from a rather unusual cup. He acquired it in Tibet. It is fashioned from the top of a Buddhist monk's skull and is encrusted with semi-precious gems. It has a silver lip.

Using such a cup is meant to remind the ritual drinker that all men, no matter how holy, can expect death.

Genghis Khan was famous for fashioning drinking vessels from the skulls of his enemies. He likely had a hell of a lot of cups.

We can use the cups made from the rich to remind ourselves not to be too greedy.

Handicrafts

There is a noticeable obsession with pre-industrial arts and crafts where I live in Central America. Retired expat women gather to weave, using hand frames. Some make baskets or artifacts from glass and stone.

We could use some of the bones of the rich to fashion craft items, such as hairpins, snuff spoons and the like. The art of scrimshaw could be practiced on larger thigh bones.

A Witches' Brew

- with profuse apologies to Shakespeare and none to those going in the pot.

First witch	Thrice the fat cat hath mewed
Second witch	Thrice and once Cameron's pig whined
Third witch	Harpier cries, tis time, tis time
First witch	Round about the caldron go; in the rich's entrails throw. Murdoch toad, that under cold stone Days and nights has thirty-one Sweltered venom sleeping got, Boil thou first i' the charmed pot.
All	Double, double toil and trouble; Fire burn and caldron bubble.

Second witch   Fillet of a banker snake,
                      In the caldron boil and bake;
                      Eye of Newt (Gingrich) and toe of Cruz,
                      Tin ear of Christie, add more booze.

                      Clinton's lies and Rubio's schlong,
                      Rand Paul's leg and Huckabee's song,
                      For a charm of powerful trouble,
                      Like a hell broth boil and bubble.

All   Double, double toil and trouble;
                      Fire burn and caldron bubble.

Third witch   Scale of Koch, tooth of Carson
                      Bush's mummy, evil parson
                      From the murderer Tony Blair,
                      cut a lock of pubic hair.

                      Root of hemlock digg'd i' the night,
                      add a gob of Osborne's spite,
                      Silvered in the moon's eclipse,
                      Nose of Biden, Kardashian's lips,

                      Ditch delivered by a drab (I see Nancy Pelosi here.)
                      Make the gruel thick and slab
                      Add thereto Putin's claws, Assad's sneers
                      and Obama's wars.

All   Double, double toil and trouble;
                      Fire burn and caldron bubble.

Second witch   Cool it with Trump's blood,
                      Then our charm is firm and good.

Health Warning

This a fantasy menu and useful only for producing politicians getting on your nerves gas. Not to ingested.

OUR DESSERTS

"Promises and pie-crust are made to be broken"
Jonathan Swift

A Problem

There is not much that is sweet about the rich. Generally, their entitled meanness requires the addition of vast amounts of sweetness to make them palatable. Sugar is bad for us. Too much honey is sickly and artificial sweeteners either taste terrible or are full of nasty chemicals.

Furthermore, few desserts are made from meat. Consequently, this section is short. Ice cream and chocolate desserts are very popular and suitable recipes are widely available if you wish to skip this section.

Rich Mince pies

Traditional English mince pies were and still are required Christmas fare. The proper way to make them is to include minced meat as below.

Ingredients

- A large jar of mincemeat
- ¼ pound of minced rich person
- ¼ cup of candied orange peel
- Icing sugar for dusting
- 1 packet of plain pastry
- ¼ cup of plain flour
- cooking oil spray

Method

1. Roll out the pastry and dust with flour on both sides. Spray non-stick bun trays with oil and using a cookie cutter line the bottoms of the trays with pastry, allowing a ¼ inch of the pastry to rise above the tray for each pie bottom.

2. Fry the meat in oil till any fat runs off and the meat is brown all over.

3. Mix the meat, the mincemeat and orange peel by hand and put a heaped tablespoonful into each pie bottom in the tray.

4. Using a smaller cookie cutter make the pie tops and seal to the now filled bottoms. Using a knife make 3 cuts per pie in the top.

5. Heat the oven to 400F and bake for 30 minutes.

6. Remove pies from the trays and allow to cool. Serve with a dusting of icing sugar.

Extremely Rum Babas

Babas are Hindu holy men and aesthetes. Hordes of them gather annually at Varanasi for their devotions.

Most are very poor and devout. These do not qualify for our menu. They walk naked, smeared with white ash and grow their hair long. Some do rather fun things, which I have never been tempted to emulate. For example, one ties several bricks to his penis and swings them about. Others are buried alive for long periods or meditate cross-legged on high poles.

There is a rapacious minority, which may be labeled as 'false prophets'. They amass great wealth, line up their devotees for sex and indulge in other chicanery. These are well worthy of a recipe.

As a boy, my father introduced me to rum babas. I liked them. Now, I just drink the rum. The recipe below is nothing like my boyhood delights.

Ingredients

- ½ pound of selfraising flour
- ¼ teaspoonful of salt
- 1 heaped tablespoonful of sugar
- 2 eggs beaten

- ¼ cup of milk
- ¼ pound of butter
- ¼ pound of very finely minced false baba meat precooked
- ½ pound of caster sugar
- ¼ cup of navy rum
- 8 ounces of double cream
- 4 ounces of icing sugar
- Fresh strawberries and blueberries to garnish

Method

1. Mix the flour, sugar, milk, eggs and butter, as if making a cake.

2. Knead this dough and combine with the minced false baba.

3. Place in a bowl and cover with clingfilm, allowing the dough to rise.

4. Grease and sugar 6 fluted savarin moulds.

5. Knead the dough and add to the moulds.

6. Bake in a preheated oven for 25 minutes at 350F.

7. Whilst baking, put the caster sugar and rum in a small saucepan and bring to a boil for only a second.

8. Place the cooked babas on plates and pour the syrup (rum and sugar) over them. Allow them to cool and turn them over once to allow the syrup to soak in.

9. Whip the cream and icing sugar and add to the top of each baba. Garnish with the fresh fruit.

Chocolate Covered Politician's Bacon

As there is so much pork in American politics, it seems only fitting that some legislators' body parts should be cured as bacon and used in this delicious dessert. David Cameron and past members of the Bullingdon club at Oxford are rumored to have an unnatural affinity with pigs, so they could be justly substituted too.

Ingredients

- 20 rashers of smoked politician's bacon with the rind cut off. (They have thick skins.)
- 12 ounces of melted dark sweetened chocolate
- Candied orange peel, very finely chopped

Method

1. Grill the bacon until crisp, draining off the fat.

2. Coat each rasher all over in the chocolate and place on a greaseproof surface.

3. Crumble the orange peel over the chocolate. Chill in the fridge.

4. Serve when set.

Blue Blood Pudding

Blood pudding is an old recipe usually made from pig's blood. Royal blood is in no way special, but will substitute well, as the royals have porcine habits and in several cases looks.

Ingredients

- 1 pint of royal blood
- 2 pounds of suet
- 1 cup of seedless sultanas
- 1 cup of sugar
- ½ cup of diced dates
- ½ cup of warmed syrup or jam

Method

1. Mix the blood, suet, sultanas, sugar and dates into a dough and place into a traditional pudding cloth, tying the top tightly. You can add some diced human sultanas if you wish.

2. Cover with water in a large pan and boil slowly for 3 hours.

3. Remove from the cloth, place on a plate.

4. Serve with the warm syrup or jam poured over the top.

Etonian Mess

Eton mess is normally a tasty concoction of meringue and strawberries. It is associated with an annual cricket match between the exclusive British private schools Eton and Harrow.

Because Tory Cabinet posts are dominated by Eton chums, Eton Mess is a good description of the state of the UK today. We have developed this new version called Etonian Mess made from UK cabinet members. We could also have called it Cabinet Pudding, but there is already another dish of that name.

Ingredients

- I punnet of strawberries
- 1 spoonful of sugar
- 1 glass of port wine
- 5 smashed meringues
- ½ pint of whipped cream
- 4 rashers of chocolate-covered politician's bacon from an earlier recipe, finely chopped

Method

1. Mash the strawberries with the sugar.

2. Gently stir in the other ingredients.

3. Serve.

Vegetarian Recipes

"A man can live and be healthy without killing animals for food, therefore, if he takes eats meat for the sake of his appetite, his act is immoral"

Leo Tolstoy

Save animals, eat the 1%

There are no cannibal vegetarian dishes silly!

Epilogue

'Our life dreams the Utopia. Our death achieves the ideal.'

Victor Hugo

Do not lose this book.

Imagine the future importance of this book. Keep it handy for after the Revolution.

Victor Hugo was partly right about death achieving Utopia, but it will be the death of the rich that does so. These recipes will help lead to it.

There will be no private aircraft, mega-yachts, flashy cars and trying to show off status and wealth with conspicuous consumption. In a flash, fear of being eaten will accomplish this planet-saving change in social attitudes.

The poor will be well fed and gradually fade from the statistics. The possessions of the greedy 1%, who currently own the world's wealth, can be redistributed.

Have no fear about a shortage of the supply of human meat. 1% of the current population is about 70 million people. The marvelous thing about percentages is that when the population drops by 70 million, there will still be a 1% of the richest to provide toothsome sustenance to the rest.

There will be some unfortunate changes in sexual behavior. Oral sex will be seen as risky rather than risqué. French kissing might give a whole new meaning to the expression 'tongue in cheek'. These minor sacrifices seem but a small price to pay for a new social order.

The beneficial consequences of cooking the rich are almost too difficult to imagine. Politicians will be honest and in short supply as few will volunteer.

Athletes will compete for the honor and the sport rather than to become rich. Children will be determined that their parents leave them little inheritance. Tax collection will become easy. Entrepreneurs and business leaders will work for fun and a living wage rather than to screw everyone else.

More from the Yarn of the Nancy Bell by W.S. Gilbert

"For a month we'd neither wittles nor drink,
Till a-hungry we did feel.
So we drawed a lot and accordin' shot
the captain for our meal.

The next lot fell to the Nancy's mate
and a delicate dish he made;
Then our appetite with the midshipmite
we seven survivors stayed.

And then we murdered the bo'sun tight
and he much resembled pig.
Then we wittled free, did the cook and me
on the crew of the captain's gig."

POSTSCRIPT

Why I wrote this book (because despite their best efforts, my wife, lawyers and friends could not stop me).

For those who like to understand why pen is put to paper, or in these times why finger is applied to computer key, or in this case why the 1% are condemned to the pot, here is the improbable explanation. The simpler one is that I am just nuts.

The political and anti-clerical ideas described in these pages have various origins. My grandfather was a jolly fellow. He was a quiet atheist, rarely roused to angry voice. The site of fat clergymen eating in expensive hotels, glanced through a window as the old man walked through the town, moved him to paroxysms of fury.

Politicians who promised everything to working class voters and delivered nothing but war and hardship were another of his bête noirs. He passed some of this to me.

My intense and often painful education at the hands brutal Catholic nuns and monks added to my cannibalistic feelings.

Observing the workings of politics and business at the highest levels and on an international scale as an investment banker, partner in a large consulting organization and later as CEO and President of a global company, confirmed my earlier views and led to considerable self-disgust and a wish to make amends.

I have always had a Monty Pythonesque sense of humor and mischievous disrespect for authority.

Lastly, it seemed time to try a new genre. I have written four volumes of fiction so far and have others in the pipeline. They are precursors leading up to this Culinary Triumph.

'*They deserved it*' is a historical novel with anti-clerical and feminist messages.

'*Revolution*' is a thriller describing events leading to and after a bloody revolution beginning in the UK and spreading internationally.

'*Terminated*' is a Thriller in two volumes, one is already available and the other is in progress. It describes the rising of a poor boy from Glasgow, his heroic deeds in the Falklands war, his success in the corrupt world of business and his transformation into the serial killer of his former business colleagues.

'*Doom Gloom and Despair*' is a collection of dark short stories most of them tongue-in-cheek. Two include cannibalism and three propose ways of resolving the current crisis of over-population and humanity's plague on the planet.

My blog at Penmanhouse.com includes poetry and other ventures into different types of writing. Now seemed the perfect time to write this spoof cookbook.

What beta readers said about this outrageous book

'Excellent, I wish I had written it' Aaron Aalborg

'Help! Save me from this madman.' Mrs. Aalborg

'He ought to be horsewhipped' Brigadier Chumbly Blimp-Farquarson

'Dinnae eat me and mi wee wifie.' The Laird of Glen Morruchty

'Kill him!' Prince Bin Lardy, Bin that book, Bin Abdul Aziz

'We are not amused.' Some old biddy from Windsor castle

'May his willy shrivel and a plague cause his living body to rot.' A curse laid on the author by the Joint Council for Ecumenical Relations.

'There is an inexorable insane logic to all this. I think he had a mother complex. Maybe I prescribed too much Adderall?' Kozibottom von Funzhaven, Aaron Aalborg's psychiatrist.

'Buy up every copy, until Amazon runs out of ink' What Aaron wishes some billionaire would say to his minions.

On behalf of the author and Penman House Publishing, thank you. We appreciate your support.

Reviews are the life's blood of publishers, authors and help inform other readers and act as signposts on the literary landscape.

Please take a moment and leave a review of this book on Amazon, GoodReads or wherever readers gather.

About the Author

Aaron Aalborg is the penname of a writer with many and sometimes strange experiences. He chooses to remain anonymous. Born in the North of England, he has variously been a trainee monk, a student activist, a Royal Marine Commando, a visiting Professor at a European Business School and a successful businessman and global CEO and finally a proponent of disturbing ideas.

He and his wife have lived in Asia, Europe and the US and travelled to all the major and some smaller countries, doing business in most of them. Until recently currently he lived in Central America. Currently he is in hiding in the mountains of Papua New Guinea.

Other Books from This Author

They Deserved It – Currently available- A novel of lust and Revenge Spanning the Centuries

What is the mysterious Egyptian casket that links murderers over a thousand years?

This thriller begins as a historical novel set in 17th Century Italy, a time of superstition, plagues and cynical exploitation of young women.

It is a ripping yarn of illicit love, hundreds of poisonings, the inquisition, torture and witch burnings, built around true events.

Characters include: Beautiful girls oppressed by dynastic marriages to aged husbands, an attractive and tormented young priest, Machiavellian cardinals and a scheming, atheist pope.

In the second part of the story, the descendants of some of the original characters are driven to fulfil their ancestral destiny in modern day New York. The results include grisly killings, global pursuit, international espionage and a thrilling climax of mass murder, authorized by the President of the United States.

It is up to you to decide which of the victims deserved their fate.

Revolution – Available Now- A thriller to change the world.

This is a must read novel for anyone who really wants to change the way the world is run. It describes a violent revolution in the near future. It begins in the United Kingdom and blossoms into worldwide mayhem.

Three radical students were radicalized in the late 1960s, but after violent experiences bide their time till they are in positions of power. In They assassinate members of the British Royal family and world leaders, before seizing control in a series of credible and stunning acts of violence.

Counter revolutionaries attempt to strike back. This is a frighteningly realistic view of what could happen in today's uncertain and dangerous times. It is of compelling interest to those of the political left and right, military specialists, radical economists and all those who enjoy a twisting turning plot with many surprises.

Terminated Volume1- From the Slums to the Falklands War- Currently Available

Revelations from recently declassified government archives drive the start of this thriller in two parts. Alex, a talented lad from the most deprived part of Scotland, overcomes the disadvantages of his birth to play a key role in Britain's victory over Argentina in the Falklands war.

He also becomes a successful businessman. The corruption and evils of corporate life are exposed through a series of exciting events.

Terminated is for those who like cliff hanging thrillers and any-one interested in the world of big business, management con-sulting and war.

Terminated Volume 2- Expected in 2016

Thwarted by sociopathic colleagues and corrupt partners, Alex turns his expertise in killing to hunting down and murdering those who fire him, over a number of years and in a variety of painful and unexpected ways.

The exposure of the dark realities of the corporate world con-tinues. The reader has to judge Alex's actions, character flaws and whether the surprising ending is justified.

This is bedtime reading for serial killers.